SPOO
STORIES

SOME TRUE, SOME NOT

MARJORIE TAVOULARIS

Printed in the United States of America.

Library of Congress Control Number: 2021908997

ISBN	Paperback	978-1-64803-650-7
	eBook	978-1-64803-651-4

Westwood Books Publishing LLC
11416 SW Aventino Drive
Port Saint Lucie, FL 34987

www.westwoodbookspublishing.com

CONTENTS

INTRODUCTION AND ACKNOWLEDGMENTS

This collection of tales has an eclectic history. Some are stories told to me by patients while I was in medical practice. Some are purely figments of my imagination while others, though imaginary, are based on experiences that I or others have had. For example, "The Burglar" originated from my imagination after my daughter and her husband were burglarized in the very fashion I describe. Fortunately for everyone concerned the felon was caught and is cooling his heels in a California prison. Some of these stories, although fictitious, are based on the mentality of inmates I came to know while I was a psychiatrist in various prisons around the States. In each case I will try to identify the source of the material. Of course, I cannot vouch for the "actual" truth of stories told to me by friends, acquaintances, or former patients. But I can reasonably attest to the fact that these stories are based on the tellers' experiential reality. That is likewise the case in the first story in this anthology: "Grandfather." It was the reality I experienced personally at the age of seven years. Because it involves my first and only "ghost" sighting and because it happened to me, I am comfortable sharing with my readers the various ways I have examined this experience.

I owe much credit for this collection of stories to the many contributors who were willing to share their experiences with me. Thanks to my colleagues in the Scottdale Writers Group for their support, encouragement, and constructive criticisms. And I want to thank the numerous correctional inmates who allowed me to get "into" their heads.

The late Francis Bambrey, a Scottdale police officer, in whose former home I wrote many of these stories, deserves credit. Those of you familiar with Scottdale years ago know that Mr. Bambrey's girth could do some serious thumping. And, as I typed, he thumped about upstairs. I would like to think Mr. B's spirit approves of my work, but-----. Most of the credit for completing and compiling this collection of stories belongs to my daughter, Diana, who proofread, made suggestions for editing, and was always, always, encouraging. This book is dedicated to Diana, who died in 2017 from complications of diabetes mellitus.

GRANDFATHER

This is the one story in this series of short stories that I can say with certainty is true, because it happened to me.

The summer I turned seven I saw what I am sure was the ghost of my paternal grandfather. He had died the previous year after a long illness. At the time I lived in Scottdale with my parents in a tenement-type apartment building owned by my grandparents. Many residents of Scottdale still call that building the Osterwise Apartments. Nowadays it is deteriorating with age and neglect, but I have a fondness for the pleasures it provided me as a child.

Before his death grandpa lived with grandma on the first floor of the building and our family lived on the third floor, which was the top floor. Steps led up to the roof from a hallway on the third floor; the roof itself was flat with two-foot walls around the sides. The door leading from the top of the stairwell to the roof was wooden and fastened only by a hook latch.

When my older sisters were home, one or the other would occasionally take me up on the roof to sunbathe. It was fun to lie in the sun, watching clouds change shape as they moved. I would imagine one was an elephant and another was a kitty cat.

On a sunny day in June of 1945 it happened that none of my sisters was home, but I wanted to go up on the roof and watch the clouds. I knew there would only be:

"No!!!"

If I begged permission from my mother. She considered the roof to be too dangerous for me unless I had adult supervision. But mother was busy that day washing clothes in the kitchen, the wringer washer noisily agitating and stationary tubs filled with rinse water containing bluing.

So, with her involved and distracted, I decided to seize the day and go up on the roof. After telling my mother that I was going down to visit with Joan Swift, my friend who lived on the second floor, I tiptoed down the hallway leading to the roof stairwell and began a stealthy ascent. After climbing about six steps I looked up to the roof door to judge how much farther I had to walk. And that is when I saw my grandfather!

He was sitting on the top step with his back to the door that accessed the roof. He was wearing the white pajamas with the blue oval design that I remembered him wearing during his final illness. His body seemed to be glowing in a pale blue haze. And he was staring right at me. In order to go out onto the roof I would have to walk right through him! Although I was only seven, I knew that my grandfather was dead and that what I was looking at was his ghost. Heart racing, I backed down the stairs, keeping my eyes on his figure, hoping he wouldn't chase after me. When I reached the bottom of the steps I made a beeline for the kitchen and the safety of my mother. The moment I reached her, I gasped breathlessly,

"Mom, Grandpa is up on the back stairs!"

She gave me a distracted look and said,

"Don't be silly. He is up in Uniontown with your Aunt Annie."

I knew she was referring to her father, still very much alive. And I knew that I had best not press the issue, because it would only lead to my getting into trouble with her for even going near the stairs leading to the roof.

And I can tell you, I never again tried going up on the roof. My sisters would invite me but I always made excuses not to go up there. And for many years the only person I ever told about my experience was my best friend and cousin, Patty.

But after I grew up, I realized that at such a young age I did not appreciate the dangers of going up on that roof. I have been told that I was the apple of my grandfather's eye. Did he come back that day to protect me from my seven year old impulsivity? Did I create my grandfather as an external projection of my guilt for planning to break a major "no-no"? Or is there another explanation for my hallucination?

THE PILLOW

The woman who told me this story is highly respected in the field of mental health. Because she was afraid that someone would think she was a bit odd, she was reluctant to share her story. After assuring her of anonymity I was able to get her to agree to allow me to include this in the book.

When I moved to California and purchased an older house, I needed to do a lot of redecorating. For my bedroom I bought a four-poster king-sized bed and made a bedspread, pillow shams and window valances. I picked out a powder-blue material with a swirled mauve design from a specialty shop in town. The final products looked lovely in the bedroom. And the fact that they were made by me and unique in their design made it all the more painful when, several years later, finances required that I sell the house.

I moved to a small apartment where my bed wouldn't fit. There was only one window in my new bedroom, and it required a full drape, not just a valance. So, I packed away the bedspread and valances but kept the shams and used them to cover pillows for my new twin-sized bed.

One day, my boyfriend Sam asked if he might take one of the pillows from my bed to use in his apartment. I was reluctant to give up the sham. But he admired my choice of material and said that was why he wanted that particular pillow.

I agreed, albeit reluctantly. And I was glad I had, when, a year or so later, Sam was killed in an automobile collision. As his daughter and I cleaned out his apartment I saw no sign of my pillow sham and gave it up for lost.

Five years later, on the anniversary of his death, I was thinking of him and reminiscing as I drove along a residential street in town. I saw an object on the road and stopped. There was a pillow with my sham! Where had it been for the past five years? And how did it get in the middle of a street where I happened to be driving?

It was the anniversary of Sam's death and he was on my mind at the time. Coincidence? I don't think so. I think Sam was returning the borrowed item and telling me that death is not the end for us.

THE FUNERAL

The woman who told me of her experience at "the funeral" has always been sensible and not taken to flights of fancy. So, I was both surprised and taken aback by this report of her experience.

I really didn't want to attend the funeral service. All the wailing of the grieving and the somber monotones of the minister make me twitchy. To add to it all, the young man who'd been killed had been driving drunk and had a reputation even at the callow age of twenty-two as a charming, handsome ne'er-do-well. But I worked as a minor administrator in the same office as his mother, a clerk-typist whom I found conscientious and dedicated to our shipping company. Thus, I found myself outside the cemetery chapel in the midst of a crowd of strangers. Most of the attendees were young adults, probably acquaintances of the deceased.

So I entered the chapel, took a seat near the rear, and listened to an organ mutedly playing "Abide With Me." As more people entered the chapel air seemed stuffy. I began hacking, the legacy of my thirty years of cigarette smoking. A dry cough seemed to plague me when I found myself in a close, quiet location. Usually this happened when I went to the cinema or was in a business meeting. I could not allow myself to disturb the service and so I slipped outside.

Across the road was a group of maple trees, and I hurried over to their leafy shelter. As I recovered from yet another fit of coughing, I found I was not alone. A young man with a shock of auburn hair and a crooked grin was leaning against one of the trees and smoking.

"If my cigarette is causing you to cough, I guess I can move," he offered with a shrug.

"Please don't bother," I replied. "My coughing is caused by the cigarettes I used to smoke, not the one you are puffing on. Although you would be wise to give them up. Actually, it feels good to have some company right now. I have been feeling a bit awkward because I didn't know the young man who died. I am just a work colleague of his mother. Are you a friend or a relative?"

"Neither," he replied, as he leaned down to brush a fleck of lint from his trousers. "I knew David well but I didn't like him. But it's expected of me to attend and so here I am."

"I've been told it is not polite to speak ill of the deceased," I replied stiffly.

"Oh, give me a break," he laughed with a degree of bitterness. "I've been told it isn't nice to lie, either! David stole money from his sister. Then, when he was evicted from his flat, he wheedled an invitation to stay at his brother's apartment, then helped himself to Sam's CD player, which he fenced. During the service you'll probably hear him referred to as a lovable rogue, but that's a kindlier moniker than he deserves. He even stole the Saab he managed to wrap around that telephone pole Saturday night."

"Well, I wouldn't know," I replied, feeling decidedly uncomfortable. I did not want to agree with this brash fellow, but I had heard similar comments from one of my co-workers the day after the accident.

"It's all right, lady. You're a friend of David's mother and she wouldn't want to hear him be criticized, either. I'd better get back inside."

And on that note, he crushed the cigarette under his heel and walked away.

I knew I should go back inside also, but I couldn't bring myself to do so. I listened from the safety of the trees as the minister's inaudible mumbling yielded to the strains of "Amazing Grace." My coughing recurred with a vengeance, so I gave myself permission to remain out in the cool spring air. When the small crowd stumbled out of the chapel I meandered over to mill with the others, who were chatting quietly in the hushed tones required at such a time. And I overheard a middle-aged matron utter, barely audibly, to her male companion, "Margaret will be better off in the long run. David gave her nothing but worry, and it would have only continued. But his tendency to call a spade a damndable spade was amusing at times and I loved his gorgeous red hair."

I never saw a picture of David and I never discussed him, or my cemetery chat, with anyone. I don't want to be thought of as a demented old woman by others or as a nut case to myself. Anyway, there are probably other red-headed young men in town who tend to be more direct than tactful. Aren't there?

THE THEATER

This experience was had by a local woman in the 1950s, when the now Geyer Theater was called the Strand Theater and was a movie house.

On Saturdays when I was in grade school, I would go to the movies with my friend Joan. Sometimes we would go to the Arcade to see cowboy movies but usually we would go to the Strand Theater to see whatever was playing. We both loved movies, no matter what was featured. But when I was in the eighth grade Joan became ill with Hodgkin's disease and died. I missed her a lot and had no friend who enjoyed the movies as much as she had.

One evening I agreed, reluctantly, to go to the movie with my mother. I don't recall what was playing, but I remember that the theater was crowded, so it must have been a popular film.

Not long after the lights dimmed and the previews came on, I felt a tremor, as though a mild earthquake was occurring. I looked around to see if anyone else was concerned and realized I was alone in the theater. That is, I was alone save a person sitting in the seat to my right. It was Joan! She told me she missed me, was lonely, and wanted me to come with her. I was scared; I told her I missed her a lot, too. But because she was dead, I would have to die also, if I were to come with her—and I didn't want to die!

Joan seemed to be disappointed and saddened, but accepted my decision. I felt another tremor and found that I was still sitting in the darkened movie theater with my mother in the seat to my left. I looked around and the crowd was back. Everyone but me seemed to be paying attention to the screen.

I never told anyone about that experience. I suppose I just dozed off. But what if?

THE BURGLAR

Although fiction, this tale is based on an actual burglary experienced by my daughter and her husband a few years ago. To the best of my knowledge the burglar, a career criminal, is still safely ensconced in a state prison.

Nicholas was a most talented burglar. Just ask him. His specialty was cleaning out suburban houses. Nowadays it seems like most families in suburbia have both parents working, which suited Nicholas just fine. And the few women who weren't gainfully employed spent hours each day at the gym or in a nail salon. So, on most days, once he gained entrance, Nicholas had the house to himself for at least two hours. Not that he needed that much time. Nicholas had a great system. He'd choose one of the upscale neighborhoods in Greensburg, Pennsylvania that boasted of roomy, split-level houses with stucco facades and landscaped back yards enclosed by high wooden fences. The hardest part of Nicholas' job was finding a house with no alarm system. To minimize his chances of discovery, Nicholas would pose a polltaker and approach his target house with a pad and paper. If anyone answered the door, he queried the occupants' political opinions and moved on to find another house that was not protected by a burglar alarm. Having found a likely one, Nicholas then approached the houses on either side of the "target" in the same manner. Only when Nicholas found three unoccupied houses in a row did he proceed. He couldn't believe how stupid folks could be. First, he'd walk into the back yard of the middle house. At least two times out of ten he found a window or door unlocked. Otherwise he'd break one of the rear windows or patio doors. Once he gained entry Nicholas could clean out a house of jewelry, credit cards, and small electronic games within fifteen minutes. He had no need to carry equipment other his notepad, pencil and a pocket-sized glasscutter. He used luggage he found within the house itself to pack his loot and carry it out to his car.

But today Nicholas was unlucky, his activity noted by a suspicious neighbor who lived across the street from the "target" house. But, of course, Nicholas did not know this and therefore he proceeded in his usual fashion.

A quick assessment of the expensive Danish Modern furnishings and an original oil painting on the living room wall confirmed Nicholas' belief that the owners of the house were Yuppie slaves to "the system" and felt innately superior to people like Nicholas--people who didn't dress in the latest fashion or use proper grammar. But Nicholas would have the last laugh by making a sizable income from fenced jewelry that belonged to the smart-asses.

There was a Cocker Spaniel napping on the bed in the master bedroom; but the dog was a lover, not a fighter, and looked bewildered when Nicholas woke him. And he licked Nicholas' hand when he gave the animal a piece of the hamburger he'd brought with him for just such an eventuality. Quickly he located the owners' suitcases in a hall closet and began filling them with items that he could fence easily. After cleaning out the woman's jewelry box he began packing Hummel figurines.

But then Nicholas heard excited chatter outside the front of the house. A glance out the living room window revealed a black-and-white and a skinny pale-faced cop standing on the sidewalk engrossed in conversation with a Preppy-looking guy. Nicholas hurried to the pull-down ladder in the hallway and climbed into the attic. He pulled up the ladder after himself and slipped under a pile of unused insulation and a tarp that had been left over after some paint job. He heard the front door opening and a distant voice say,

> "Are you sure the prowler came into my house?" An authoritative voice answered,

> "Look, Sir, we need to check this out and we'd like you to go back outside and wait."

Nicholas wished fervently that the cop would not think to look in the attic. The place was hot as Hades and he itched unmercifully from the insulation. But after a period of time Nicholas heard steps on the creaky pull-down and a voice, now quite near to him said,

> "OK, asshole, come out of there. I know you're hiding under that stuff."

Nicholas' heart was banging against his ribcage and he had to hold his breath to keep from gasping. Then he remembered that he had brought a gun with him to frighten into submission anyone he found inside the house. He eased the gun from his jacket pocket. He debated whether or not to try to shoot it out with the cop. Another arrest now would lead to a "third strike" conviction and he was unwilling to spend the rest of his life in prison.

After deciding that there was only one cop with him in the attic and realizing that the cop couldn't know for sure that he was under the pile of insulation, Nicholas lay without moving, listening and waiting. Maybe the officer would decide that he had already escaped or was hiding somewhere downstairs. But then he heard the cop, talking on his two-way radio, say,

"The SOB is up here in the attic under a pile of junk and won't come out. Call for a K-9 unit."

That did it. Nicholas was not going to wait to be chewed on. He let loose a barrage of bullets in the direction of the cop's voice.

There was only silence after the gunfire stopped; Nicholas lay motionless. But then he realized he'd better get out of there before the K-9 unit arrived. He hurried down the ladder but heard talking outside. He glanced out the living room window and saw a Westmoreland County police sedan. A young cop was standing on the sidewalk.

Nicholas hurried to the pull-down ladder and climbed up into the attic. He buried himself under a pile of unused insulation and a tarp. The place was hot and he was itchy. All was silent. He got out from under the stuff, pushed the ladder, climbed down and went back into the living room. A glance out the picture window revealed a uniformed cop standing on the sidewalk outside his patrol car.

Nicholas rushed to the hallway, pulled down the ladder and climbed up and back under the insulation material. He began to itch.

In the living room an attractive couple in their mid-thirties was watching Jeopardy on television. The woman said,

"David, if I didn't know better, I'd swear we have a ghost. Ever since the police shot and killed that burglar, I have been hearing sounds as though someone is moving around in the attic."

BOB'S DREAM

The following "dream" seems to have been more than the illogical ramblings of the unconscious mind. This was told to me by a woman I worked with and I never saw any evidence that she was other than a sane and sensible person.

When I began dating Bob, I was still reeling from a broken marriage. Bob seemed to be sensitive and caring and I was hungry for the sort of attention he provided me. So, when he told me that he had recently been paroled from prison I was only mildly shaken.

He told me that he had come from Florida to visit his father, had gotten involved with some shady men who were not only drug dealers but also were politicians in the town where his father lived. He said that when he tried to extricate himself from the drug activity he was "set up" and ended up a felon, serving time in a state penitentiary. He added that now, even though he was paroled, the drug scions would not rest until he was dead. When he told me this, I could tell he was frightened. But I was convinced that these evil men were surely satisfied that he had been "put away" for a few years. As our relationship blossomed, I put Bob's fears out of my mind; I had convinced myself that he was in no danger.

A few months later about one o'clock in the early morning, alone in my house, I was jolted awake with the "realization" that I was in danger of being shot. At the time I reacted totally out of character for me. I got up, went to my kitchen, got a butcher knife and proceeded to check every room in my house for an intruder. I made sure all of my windows and doors were locked and then went outside and walked the perimeter of my property, looking for any signs of invasion. Finding none, I went back into the house and lay down on a couch in my living room, listening for signs of the "attack," my knife at the ready. About three o'clock I "realized" the danger had passed, and went back to bed and slept soundly. The next day, a Friday, I pondered over the dream and was amazed when I thought about my reaction to it. I am the sort of person who, faced with an intruder, would probably cover my head with the blanket and pretend to be asleep!

Bob and I had a date scheduled for that evening but he didn't show up. This was really out of character for him. But he was living with his elderly father, and I considered that the old man may have taken ill. When I called his home, there was no answer; and I never heard from Bob the next day.

But as I read the Saturday newspaper, I read that a fellow from the town where Bob lived had been shot in the head and was on life support. Fearing the worst, I drove to the hospital and went to the ICU, where I found Bob's dad sitting in a bit of a daze. Eventually I uncovered the tale of what had happened: Bob had gone out Thursday evening after receiving a phone call. He told his father he would be home by midnight. But his father heard nothing until about three o-clock in the morning, when a sound outside caused him to open his door. There he found Bob convulsing on the ground. The old man called 911 and followed the ambulance to the hospital. He was told an hour later that Bob was in surgery and that he had been shot by a high-powered rifle. The police were investigating but no one could account for Bob for the two hours prior to the shooting.

Bob died on Saturday. On Tuesday morning as I drove to the funeral I was grieving and inattentive. So when I found myself stuck behind a slow-moving semi I determined to pass the truck, forgetting that the road on which I was driving was only a two lane road. As I pulled into the left lane I realized that there was another truck coming toward me! I pulled back in behind the semi but lost control of my car and, as though I were taking Mr. Toad's Wild Ride, I wobbled and veered all over both lanes of the highway, As this road insanity was occurring I could "see" Bob in my mind's eye, sitting in the passenger seat beside me. He told me I must not get injured because I was the only person who could help solve his murder. And he said,

"Brake now!"

I did so. Somehow, no other car was in my path as my car turned one hundred eighty degrees and flew sideways into the adjacent field. The wheels of my car were knocked off but the chassis, instead of overturning, dropped upright onto the grassy field. I was unhurt.

Reflecting later, I believe I was "channeling" Bob's emotions for the hour or two before he was shot and that my reactions were not mine but Bob's. I have never found a way to help solve Bob's murder. But recently I read that several corrupt politicians in his town had been convicted of drug trafficking and are headed to prison. I bet Bob is up there laughing

AROMAS

These experiences with various smells were told to me by a young relative who seems otherwise to be "normal."

There are several odors which I associate with people close to me who have passed on. These aromas have occurred at times and in places where there is no possibility of a reasonable explanation. I suspect that the smells are evidence of spirit visitations from my family. None of these visitations seem to be harbingers of problems. I have concluded that my family is just dropping by to remind me that they are still around and aware of my comings and goings.

1) The most common smell for me is that of cigar smoke. My father had the smelly habit of smoking stogies and he seemed to reek of the strong tobacco. But one summer day my daughter and I were driving out in the country. All windows of the car were up, the air conditioner was blasting, and no humans were in sight. My daughter had dozed off. Suddenly I became aware of a strong odor of

cigars that I associate with my father. After about five minutes my daughter awoke and shouted,

"Grandpa!"

After that, the odor dissipated. But occasionally since that time both she and I experienced my father's "visits," which we identify by the overpowering smell of cigar smoke.

2) I have had similar "visits" from my brother, who died about ten years ago. He worked in a steel mill and would come home reeking of sweat. So, every year or two, only when I am alone, I will become aware of a strong pungent sweaty odor. After checking myself and finding no evidence of body odor I just say,

"Hi, Bill,"

and go on about my business.

3) And then there are the lilacs. My mother always wore a floral perfume that had a prominent lilac fragrance. And ever since she died, she will "visit" me, identifying herself by that special very delightful aroma.

THE WARNING DREAM

A nurse of my acquaintance told me last year of this dream and its aftermath. She still isn't sure if she believes it herself. The city and the physician's name are changed in this accounting.

A couple of years ago I dreamed that I was kissed on the back of the head by this very handsome man, who then walked to the door of my bedroom and beckoned me to follow him. I awakened aroused and a bit embarrassed. Why was I, a sixty-year-old widowed grandmother, having a sex dream? The dream stayed with me as I went through my daily chores. And I knew that the gorgeous man in my dream was Dr. Andrew Stewart, a neurosurgeon at the Baltimore hospital where I had worked as a nurse nearly forty years ago. I had had a mad crush on Dr. Stewart, and we flirted a bit. But that ended when I met John, then a resident in ophthalmology. John became the love of my life. And when he finished his residency training, we married and moved to Seattle.

John established a flourishing practice and I retired to raise our rapidly-expanding family. But right after our thirty-seventh wedding anniversary John was diagnosed with pancreatic cancer and was dead within six months. I handled my grief by joining a bridge club and spending more time with my grandchildren.

Several days after my dream, while clothes shopping with my daughter Suzy, she asked me,

> "Have you had any repercussions from that ball hitting you?"

At first I didn't even remember what she was referring to. But then I recalled that when the nine-year-old twins, Sam and Nathan, were playing catch with a mush ball a few weeks earlier I had been clobbered on the head when I stepped into the trajectory of one of the balls.

"It hurt like blazes at the time, but I didn't even have a headache the next day," I bragged.

But later that day, with Dr. Stewart still on my mind, I suddenly remembered his lecture about subdural hematomas.

"The blow may not seem like much at the time; but if a small vein between the dura mater and the brain substance is torn, blood accumulates slowly and a month or six weeks later the injured person can be in serious trouble."

But I had absolutely no symptoms of concussion, not even a headache, and I am almost certain that Dr. Stewart said that a person with a subdural hematoma would have a chronic headache. So I tried to forget about it. But both the dream of Dr. Stewart's kiss and the memory of his lecture lingered. And I couldn't help but wonder if that gorgeous fellow was still in Baltimore. After all, he probably wouldn't be more than eighty years old. Maybe I could renew an old friendship over the phone and get a curbstone consultation at the same time.

The following day I looked on the internet, found a phone listing for him, and called. The woman who answered identified herself as his housekeeper. After a brief discussion about my identity and the reason for my call, she told me that Dr. Stewart had died of a heart attack just ten days earlier.

I was numb when I hung up the phone. He must have died around the same time that I had my dream. I phoned my general physician, told him of my head injury, and sufficiently prevaricated ongoing symptoms so as to justify a CAT scan.

Well, the CAT scan showed a rather large hematoma in the occipital part of my skull, just under the area of my dream kiss. I recovered fully from the ensuing craniotomy. But not from Dr. Stewart's "visit" to me. Was he telling me that the blow to my head started a reaction that could lead to my following him—to respond to his beckoning by dying? I know it started a reaction in me that I hadn't felt in a long time and really got my attention!

TOMB TALES

One of my colleagues in the Scottdale Writer's Group has had several spooky experiences. She has graciously allowed me to include some of her stories here.

1) In the late 1980s I lived with my husband in the house that is at the corner of Chestnut Street and Broadway. My husband worked shifts so there were nights when I was alone during the night. Frequently, about 2 am, as I lay in bed, I would hear what sounded like a large group of people mumbling outside. I figured it was people leaving the American Legion, which was across the street from our house. One night I decided to walk out onto the porch and see what the folks were up to. Well, when I walked out onto the porch the Legion was dark, and the street was quiet. From that time on I decided to leave the spirits to their activities and I stayed in bed while they murmured outside.
2) One night, in the same house, while I was lying in bed waiting for my husband to come home from work, a

woman walked right along the foot of my bed. She was wearing a mint-green top and shorts, had short curly hair and looked very ill. She seemed to be solid, like a living person, but she didn't look at me and faded away as she got near the door. Later I learned that the wife of a former tenant in our house had cancer and died in the house. I have never seen a picture of her but I think I saw her that night.

3) My first husband was unfaithful and we divorced when he was forty-one years old. Four months later he died of a heart attack. A week before he died he had asked me to let him come home but I had refused. Several months later I woke in the middle of night and found him sitting on my bed crying. He said he wanted me to come with him. Frightened, I turned over in the bed and covered my head. I lay there frozen in fear but eventually fell asleep. A few months later I learned that a woman my former husband had been involved with had become ill with a rapidly-growing cancer and died. It makes me wonder if he came to her also, invited her to come with him and she took him up on it!

4) This was not personally experienced by me but was told to me by a woman in Everson whom I trust. She told me her husband's first wife made him promise before she died that he would not remarry. He promised; but

after a time he missed married life and fell in love with my friend. On their wedding night my friend awoke to find a ghostly-looking woman standing over her. The woman touched her arm and then faded away. The next morning, she had a burn mark, as though from a branding iron, on her arm in the exact spot where the wraith had touched her.

THE HEIST

This is obviously a fabrication. But it is a story that I wrote many years ago, one in a series that suggests that "bad things happen to bad people."

Nick stared at the glistening, fragmented glass with dawning awareness.

"That's not a spider web", he thought. "I'm looking at what's left of my windshield!"

He pushed the glass netting away from his face impulsively. Worriedly he looked for cuts on his hand, but there were none. A quick assessment of his arms and legs removed any concern about paralysis. It was all coming back in a rush, now. Robbing the Countryside branch of the Scottdale Bank and Trust in Mount Pleasant, the look on the teller's face when he saw the Richard Nixon mask! So what if it was October, 2008 and Tricky Dicky now dead these many years! It was Halloween, wasn't it?!! And Tricky Nick was very much alive!

The mask had waited for him in his mountain cabin ever since that first bank robbery he'd done 15 years ago. Before the cops had traced him down, before Nancy had skipped town with the remaining loot, before he put twelve years in that hellhole of a prison in Greensburg where a thug in the green uniform of a guard had smashed his nose with a side baton. Before a shrink on a power trip had tried to mess with his head. Yes, and before he managed to choke out monthly

"Yessirs"

and smile at the stupid parole agent, while dying to spit in his pimply face.

He had tolerated the fleabag hotel in Jeannette for the three years, compliments of the State Parole Department, all the while dreaming of his perfect hiding place. No one knew he had a cozy lair up in Donegal. From the outside it looked like an old abandoned storage shed and the sign,

"Danger—collapsed mine shaft,"

was enough to keep the occasional hunter away. Proof was that the only invaders he'd found after his fifteen years' absence were spiders and field mice. Of course the dirt road ended a quarter mile from the faded wood structure; but Nick was in great shape, thanks to the exercise yard at the SCF-Greensburg. This car accident would do no more than delay his reaching the safety of his cabin. Nosiree, Babe! He recalled now that he had been passing Laurelville when the rain started. And the freezing sleet had begun to fall around Bear Rocks. Bad luck for so early in the year, but the car probably hadn't left the road until he was near Acme. Even with the bag of money, he could climb up the hillside and cross Route 31, no doubt now deserted in the dusk of this early Halloween storm. The shrink at the prison had told him he had a self-defeating streak a mile wide. Well, as far as Nick was concerned that shrink had a backside a mile wide! OK. So he'd dropped his wallet in the First National Bank during the heist 15 years ago. He'd been a klutz, sure, no doubt about it. But self-defeating? Bull! And this storm wasn't his fault, was it? He had packed a heavy coat and boots in the trunk of the Mercury just to be on the safe side. He might not be a boy scout but he'd learned to be prepared. Even if he had to drag the burlap sack up the hill, he'd be able to carry it once he got up to the highway. He guessed he'd better get a move on. He didn't know how long he'd been sitting here just daydreaming, but it was time for action. A quick glance in the back seat showed the dirty white moneybag waiting for him. The roof of the Mercury was caved in on the passenger's side of the car—he must have rolled down the side of the mountain. His door was mashed and wouldn't budge. But he could hoist himself out the open rectangle that had once held his windshield. He got up on his hands and knees with ease, surprising even himself with his agility. A push on the dash and he slid through the open space like a porpoise leaping in the ocean.

"Free! Now to get the loot and be on my way"

he muttered, just before he glanced back and saw a form in the driver's seat he had just vacated. Sightless eyes stared blankly. Caked blood on the face was mixed with a cheesy gray substance Nick knew had to be brain matter. But the scar across the bridge of the nose on that lifeless body was a dead giveaway--Nick was staring at his own corpse.

COINCIDENCES

The vignettes written below were told to me by acquaintances. While not ghostly they seemed so unusual I decided to include them in these pages. The first two stories were reported by employees of a nearby prison but do not seem to require that setting to be eerily odd.

1) I am a teacher at a correctional institution for inmates serving life sentences. Usually I do not learn personal information from inmates. But one day I gave a class assignment to write a theme about something that had changed their lives. One young Hispanic man, whom I will call Miguel, wrote about how he learned not to hate all white people. He said that in second grade he jabbed his pencil into the hand of a fellow classmate, who was Caucasian. The boy had done nothing except have a white face. The teacher saw the incident, and instead of punishing Miguel, asked first that Miguel apologize, then had the boys shake hands and promise not to fight. A few days later the Caucasian boy, who I will call "Tom

Johnson", invited the Hispanic boy home for lunch, where he met Tom's mother and younger sister Marilyn. Miguel, in his theme paper, said he never became close friends with Tom, but he realized that Tom's family was not all that different from his own. Miguel's paper was well-written and I asked him to read the paper aloud to his classmates. Later that very day, after I left the prison, I went to my beautician for a haircut. Sitting in a chair across from me was a woman wearing a UPS uniform bearing the name Marilyn Johnson. As my hair stylist was cutting my hair, I asked her if she knew the UPS employee; and she said the woman was her niece, the daughter of the stylist's sister. I inquired as to whether Marilyn had a brother Tom, and she said that she did indeed, and that he was a local high school basketball coach. For reasons of confidentiality I could tell neither the hairdresser nor the inmate of the amazing coincidence but by changing the names and circumstances I feel I can talk about it.

2) Years ago, before I met my current husband, I became acquainted with a fellow—I will call him Steve--to whom I felt a strong attraction. At the time of this incident I am going to tell you about I had recently been introduced to him, although later on we did have a romance. We were both living in Fresno, California, and shared an interest

in duplicate bridge. A woman with whom I partnered in the game asked me to go to a bridge tournament in Riverside, which was a drive of about two hundred miles. So, we went together in her car, stopped for an early dinner, and then, after reaching Riverside, drove down a boulevard leading to the site of the tournament. It was dark and rainy, but as I glanced out of the car window, I had a glimpse of a man in a phone booth about a block away, down a side street. For reasons I will never be able to explain I told my friend to stop the car because Steve was out there in a phone booth, lost and calling for directions on how to get to the tournament. She stopped the car and I hurried toward the figure in the phone booth. As the rain dampened my hair and clothes I began to realize that I had no reason to think that the person in the phone booth was Steve, and that I was likely to be very embarrassed to find I was on a fool's errand. But, as I got to the booth, the door opened and Steve stepped out, shocked to see a familiar face. He said he hoped to play in the tournament but had never been in Riverside and realized he did not have the address of the scheduled tournament. He had been calling a bridge director in Fresno to try to get the information but no one had answered the phone.

VISITATION DREAM

This dream/experience was told to me by a parole agent who said she was convinced after the events in this story that she was actually visited by the spirit of her friend.

While working as a parole agent in Los Angeles I dated a fellow named Larry who taught school in the city. One day he told me that the previous evening he had met a woman with a small child crying on the street near his apartment building. He said she told him she had been evicted from her mother's house after an argument on child rearing and that she had no money for a hotel room. He offered her and her daughter the couch in his apartment for the night. Then he mentioned her name (I will call her Grace.) I was horrified. This woman was a parolee on my caseload. Larry said she told him she was on parole, and that is why he was telling me about what had transpired. I told him he had done a foolish thing--she might steal from him. And that I hoped he had not mentioned me in any way to the parolee. He assured me that he had not told her anything about me, and that she and her child had left this morning, that his apartment had not been ransacked, and he did not expect to see her again.

About six months later Larry was killed in an automobile accident. A few months later I had the following dream:

Larry and I were sitting in a coffee shop chatting. As we talked it dawned on me that he was dead. He got tears in his eyes and told me he needed a big favor from me. He needed me to tell Grace that he had really cared for her. When I awakened, the dream seemed to be foolish—I didn't think Larry had had any contact with Grace beyond that one kind but foolhardy gesture of his. By the time of my dream the parolee was no longer on parole and had moved from Los Angeles. I felt a bit insulted—had he cared for the both of us? But the vivid dream stayed with me. And I felt some sort of obligation to make contact with Grace. I even checked the parole records to see if she had left a change of address but she had not.

It must have been nearly a year later that the parole office had a problem with its fire alarm system and as a result the building had to be evacuated. When I got outside, there, walking up the street, was Grace. I went over to her and started chatting. I told her that, before he died a friend of mine told me he wanted her to know he cared about her. She looked incredulous and stared at me with a dumbfounded look, then gasped,

> "Are you talking about Larry, the school teacher?!!"

I assured her that I was. Smiling as tears ran down her cheeks, she said,

> "I didn't know he had died! And how did you know him?!! He was my light and I thought he had just blown me off without a goodbye!"

I made up some believable falsities that satisfied her. But I was reeling mentally for a long time about Larry and her and how he decided to use me as a messenger for this woman who really needed to hear from him. But I was left thinking,

> "Hey, Larry, what about me?!!"

THE JAIL INFIRMARY NURSE

This is a piece of fiction. It is based on an experience I had while working in a county jail. There was one of the control rooms that sometimes seemed to be occupied and at other times seemed empty. One day when I asked a nurse why it wasn't used all of the time, she gave me a look of incredulity and informed me that it hadn't been used for years for anything but storage!

I think if it hadn't been for Sam, I would have quit my first day on the job. I hadn't wanted to work in a jail to begin with and the orientation program for new employees only served to confirm that. But where else was I going to get a job paying $6000/ month plus free health benefits as a newly graduated nurse? Bills from school tuition were overdue and if I was going to work at all I had to pay for daycare for Stephanie. Richard and I had been separated for eighteen months, divorced since April, and I had seen not one penny of the $500 monthly child support checks I had been granted.

If you have had the good fortune to avoid jails thus far in your life, let me say that you are not missing anything of beauty. The walls are gray, the cement floors are gray. Iron gates and doors clang open and clang shut at a frequency that puts your teeth on edge. The gates and doors are opened and closed by correctional officers who sit in elevated control rooms that are encased in smoked bullet-proof glass that is tinted so darkly that one cannot see into the rooms without shading one's eyes right against the glass. Even the infirmary is gray. The holding cells have just a bed, a thin mattress, and a steel commode and sink. And "suicide cells" don't even have the bed or mattress, just a cement block bunk with a thin plastic mat.

The infirmary was my assigned base at the jail. And upon my arrival the first day I discovered that five of the eight infirmary beds were filled by inmates considered to be suicidal. I could see one swarthy Hispanic man curled on his cement bunk, sobbing. An African-American man of indeterminate age was pacing and mumbling to no one in particular. A young woman with matted and filthy blond hair was sitting on the cement floor of the cell and staring at her fingernails. Each appeared to be suffering in some private hell unknown to the rest of us. In nurses' training I had liked my psychiatric rotation. And these inmates stirred my desire to help. But just as I was considering how best to approach each inmate the head nurse commented:

> "Fortunately we don't get involved with those nuts—a psych. tech. comes around to see them. Most of our day will be spent seeing inmates that have put in requests to see the doctor. Nearly all of them are just whiners so don't let them 'con' you. They just want pain meds or 'sleepers'."

By the end of that first morning I was exhausted physically and devastated emotionally by the heartlessness of the head nurse, who seemed to have lost any sense of humanity she may have once harbored.

I begged off having lunch with her in the cafeteria by saying I had a headache and would just have a cup of coffee in the infirmary kitchen. As soon as she left the area, I walked out into the hall with plans to go to my car and have a pity party. But as I passed the control room nearest the infirmary the control room door opened and an officer motioned me to come in. He introduced himself as Sam Stevens, said he knew I was a new nurse, and that I was looking a bit stressed. I tried to pass off my tension as nothing but new employee jitters, but he drew me out, and before I could stop myself, I was reporting tearfully that I felt the inmates were being treated horribly and that I could not stand working here another day. Sam listened, and when I had finished, he told me that I was a ray of sunlight in the drab jail, and that, if I stayed with it, I would learn that there were good and bad among both inmates and staff, and that I would learn how to do my part in easing the miseries of each person who needed me, regardless of their station in life. He told me that the head nurse had been beaten by an inmate she had tried to help and that she was now guarded and closed off to protect herself. He said that I was welcome to come into the control room anytime he was there and talk over my experiences and he would be glad to help me put those experiences into the perspective of his several years of experience as a custodial officer.

When I went home that day I was filled with mixed emotions. I was still offended by the attitude of the head nurse. I had come to know that she had been traumatized by her jail experiences. But I was heartened to realize that there was at least an experienced correctional officer who didn't think I was just a soft-hearted do-gooder. As I reflected on what Sam had said to me, I knew I would stick with the job for at least my three-month probationary period.

I didn't have the opportunity to visit with Sam for the next few days but then there was another morning when I felt particularly distressed over an inmate who was dying of AIDS. And on my lunch break I peered into the control room and Sam beckoned to me. This time I paid attention to his looks, not just his kind and thoughtful manner. He was stocky, a bit taller than my 5'9", and with a face more rugged than handsome. His nose, probably broken in the past, bent slightly to the right. His hair was his most unforgettable feature--dark, straight, with a shock of white hair running back from his face just slightly off center. I recognized this as a genetic variant called piebald. When Sam saw me looking at it he smiled and said some people said it was proof that he can be a skunk. I ventilated about the inmate with the life-threatening infection and he told me that he had known that inmate ten years before as a vicious rapist who was thought to have contracted the HIV virus from one of his victims! We agreed that this was some sort of poetic justice. When I returned to work that afternoon I was able to provide nursing care to the inmate with AIDS without being overly sentimental.

During my probationary period I must have visited with Sam four or five times. Without fail he helped me put my experiences into useful perspective. I began to harbor some romantic fantasies about him, despite the fact that he seemed to treat me like a kid sister. I decided that the next time I had a chance to talk with him I would try to steer the conversation into some personal areas to see what I could learn about his life outside the jail. But the next week when I peered into the control room on my lunch break it appeared cluttered with boxes and extra chairs. Sam's desk wasn't visible and it was apparent that the room had been converted into storage space.

When the infirmary officer came by a few minutes later I asked him why the control room was now being used for storage. He said it has been used for storage for at least two years, since the County cutbacks led to several officer layoffs. Although this made no sense to me, I pushed on:

> "Well, do you know where Sam Stevens is now assigned to work?"

The infirmary officer looked at me with a sardonic grin:

> "I guess he's working graveyard shift; that's where he's been hanging out since they buried him."

I realized that we must be talking about two different men and said,

> "Maybe I have the officer's name wrong. I am talking about the fellow with the white streak in his hair".

The officer said, "Well, yes, that was "Skunky" Stevens, and he was assigned to that control room a few years ago. He was killed in a car wreck on his way home from work one night about three years ago."

Needless to say, reader, I can't talk about Sam at work. I don't think I'm nuts, and I know what I experienced. I decided to tell you this story. Laugh if you want. But know that, should you ever find yourself a "guest" of the Fayette County jail and have reason to be laid up in the infirmary, there is a nurse there who will be kind to you, even if she isn't sympathetic to your criminal behavior.

RENEE'S BUTTERFLY

Renee Blasco is a member of the Scottdale Writer's Group. She has had paranormal experiences throughout her life and she has shared some of her stories with me. I am enclosing one that happened to her in early December of 2008.

Renee's elderly mother-in-law Helen died in November of 2007. The woman's youngest daughter, Kathy, had been especially close to her mother and had not been able to shake her grief and sadness.

In early December of 2008 Renee was Christmas shopping at the Marshalls Department Store in the Hempfield Plaza when she felt a tingling sensation. She glanced to her left and saw her deceased mother-in-law standing nearby, smiling and glowing. Helen was wearing a black slacks outfit with a shiny silvery top that she had worn at Christmas time while alive. Other shoppers passed by, oblivious to the drama. Once her mother-in-law had Renee's full attention she stretched out her hand toward a white box on a nearby shelf; and then she vanished.

Renee hurried to the spot where she had seen the apparition and on the shelf was a white box. Inside was a large ceramic butterfly-shaped ornament with the word, "Remember," inscribed in gold. On the back wing of the butterfly was written a poem that ended with the phrase:

"I will be there."

Renee realized that her mother-in-law wanted Kathy to have the butterfly. She sensed that Helen wanted to give Kathy a final Christmas gift and to show that a mother's love lasts beyond the grave.

As one might expect, Kathy was touched deeply by the butterfly and of Renee's tale of how she came to acquire it.

The story didn't end there. Last year, after a mass held in Mrs. Blasco's memory, a yellow butterfly landed on Renee's palm as she stood on the sidewalk outside the church. And Renee knows her mother-in-law was saying,

"I am here."

HALLOWEEN

This is a made-up story, but based on something said to me by an inmate with more brawn than intellect. He had been told by the prison board that they were going to reconsider him (probably for transfer to a different facility.) But he did not know what the word meant and came whining to me that he felt that he was in danger of being punished or even killed by prison officials. No offense is intended to the God-loving Amish, who of course carry out no such meetings as described here.

I don't like Halloween anymore. I suppose a guy could say I'm scared of it-- if he wants his lights punched out. What I really feel is more like apprehension. I get uneasy by mid-October when dark comes early, the night air has a chill, and nearly-leafless trees look gnarled like an old man twisted with arthritis. Halloween week I close up shop early, before the sun goes down. Then I high-tail it to my third-floor walk-up in one of the few still-surviving tenement buildings in Scottdale. I hole up until daylight offers a pretense of security. Each morning I venture back out to the corner of Routes 119 and

819, where I prop up my "Cold and Hungry—Will Work for Food" sign, sit on the curb, and try to look forlorn. It's not difficult; business is slow and I know that I am going to have to look for a better corner or a bigger town soon. But so far, I can pay my rent and have enough left over for my meager needs. And I usually get enough to eat from folks who are more willing to hand me a Big Mac than a buck.

But back to Halloween. When I was a kid growing up in a series of foster homes in Western Pennsylvania, I thought Halloween was the greatest. I used the night to make up for the lack of gifts on Christmas. With face paint and a loud

"BOO!"

I could scare timid kids out of their cache of candy. By the time I was sixteen and had finished a stint in the Youth Authority I realized that costume and mask gained me ready access to most mom-and-pop grocery stores open on Halloween evening. I've always had a way with words, and by flashing my Saturday night special I got enough money to live high on the hog. But in 1988 a Shop and Save clerk who had more guts than brains cold-conked me with a can of stewed tomatoes and I ended up doing a four-year stint in Cresson Prison. I used the time to improve my mind. After that, armed robbery no longer seemed to be in my best interest.

OK, back to why Halloween leaves me uncomfortable. By 1995 I was twenty-five, was skilled in the art of jewelry theft, and had made some useful connections. The poet, Robert Frost, said,

> "Good fences make good neighbors."

I say,

> "Good neighbors make good fences."

My cellie at Cresson was a good fence and when he paroled to Philadelphia we maintained our neighborliness. That was why on Halloween in 2000 I happened to be driving to Philadelphia with a bag of purloined "ice". I took Route 30 through central Pennsylvania, stopped for sauerbraten dinner (I've always loved Pennsylvania Dutch food) and then drove off for what I thought would be the final two-hour leg of the trip.

Just east of Lancaster a slow-moving horse-drawn carriage appeared ahead of me. It seemed unusual for an Amish farmer to be on the highway after dark, but there he was. For an instant I considered robbing the fellow—it would have been as simple as the times I took candy from kids. But I doubt the Amish have anything of value to me. So I just pulled out to pass. I don't know to this day whether the tail end of my Mercury clipped the wagon or if the farmer pulled his wagon into my car. All I know is, my vehicle spun out of control and rolled. No matter what anyone thinks, I was not knocked out. And everything I am going to tell you now really happened and is not a fantasy born of brain concussion. When my car stopped rolling I was trapped inside, the doorframe bent, the sedan's roof pushed down against me. Through the cracked front window, I could see the Amish farmer with his long beard and overalls. He was holding a pitchfork.

"Get help!" I yelled, but he replied,

> "Just you calm yourself young man. I have some things I want to say to you."

And he went on to list my "sins," as he called them, stressing my proclivity for taking advantage of those weaker than myself. He told me the "brethren" did not hanker to such behavior and that I needed to mend my ways. At that point I would have agreed to hand over my non-existent first-born child, because I was trapped and helpless in that cornfield. So, I promised I would be the epitome of a good citizen if he would please call for help. The farmer chuckled and commented that his folk don't use English contrivances such as cell phones. But he accepted my promise to "turn away from evil."

Then he added that the "brethren" get together each year on the evening of October 31; and that they would "reconsider" me if I reverted to type. I wasn't sure what he meant, but a cold chill of foreboding came over me. I figured I'd better ask just exactly what "reconsidering" involves. But he was no longer standing there. Instead I saw a flashlight beam and the uniform of a state trooper. For the first time in my life I was glad to see a cop. When I told him I needed to have a word with the Amish farmer, the trooper gave me an odd look. After a moment of hesitation he remarked that the only Amish farmer he'd seen that evening was the one up on the road, dead under his overturned wagon.

I never got to Philadelphia that night and haven't been there since. In fact I try to stay a fair distance west of Harrisburg. I am not always successful with my promise to live a God-fearing life. For that reason, I consider it prudent to spend Halloween nights in my apartment where--OK--where the Amish--can't "reconsider" me.

THE CHRISTMAS GHOST

The woman who told me this story lives in Latrobe and said she had this experience in a cemetery on the property of Saint Vincent's College. Although she denies experiencing anything paranormal before or since, the experience has left her with a strong interest in, and curiosity about, the afterlife. I have changed the names of the principals for obvious reasons.

The summer of 1988 seemed magical. I had turned seventeen, and my final year of high school was approaching. Penn State had given me a provisional acceptance, and Sam Waterman, the captain of the basketball team, had invited me to a July Fourth cookout.

So why was I dreaming about Christmas? For the past several nights my dreams were filled with red and green lights and silver tinsel. This made no sense to me. If any holiday should have been in my dreams it should have been Independence Day, with its parades, fireworks, and Sam.

When June twenty-eighth arrived, my mother asked me to accompany her to the cemetery by St. Vincent's College. She wanted to plant flowers on my father's grave. It would have been a happy occasion—the celebration of their twenty-five years of marriage--if Dad hadn't developed pancreatic cancer and died three years earlier. I wasn't thrilled about the cemetery venture. The loss of my father had been painful, but I had moved on as only the young can do, experiencing the thrill of anticipated adulthood. I didn't feel the need to visit his grave. Anyhow, something about cemeteries gave me the creeps. Of course, I knew that graves held only the earthly shells of the dead; and that their spirits, if there were such, weren't hanging around their bodies. But still I got goose bumps at the idea of going out to the cemetery. Nevertheless, I trotted along because I sensed Mom needed the moral support.

Except for my father, I had never known anyone else in the family to die. At the cemetery I commented to my mother about that. She said she knew I didn't remember him, but that her brother Raymond had died in the Viet Nam conflict when I was only two years old. She added,

> "He loved you dearly, and could get you giggling over the faces he made. In fact, he always called you, "Rose" because he said you were as beautiful as the flower."

As mother planted the flowers on my father's grave, I noticed a young man in military fatigues standing in the grass about the length of a football field from us. His outfit seemed dated and too warm for the weather that day. I felt he was watching us. And as I stared back at him, he beckoned. I turned back to my mother and told her to look at the fellow. But when she did so, he was no longer there. I couldn't imagine where he could have gone; there were no trees to hide behind. At this point I was curious rather than apprehensive. So when Mom finished the planting I asked her to walk down with me to the spot where I had seen the fellow. As we neared the area, my mother commented that we were close to the graves of her parents, both of whom had died in a car wreck before I was born. When we reached my grandparents' graves, I saw the rose. It was lying next to the grave of my grandmother. The tombstone on the grave which held the rose bore the inscription:

Raymond Kennedy
Beloved Son of Harold and Marilyn Kennedy
B. 12/25/50
D. 10/29/73

Now my dreams of Christmas took on a whole new meaning to me. Even though I had no actual memories of my mother's brother I knew that, wherever he was, he still remembered me fondly and was able to communicate that fact in a way his callow seventeen-year-old niece could understand.

All I said to my mother was,

> "Oh, Uncle Ray was born on Christmas!"

But in my mind, I said,

> "Hi, Uncle Ray, and thanks for the rose. You really got my attention this week. This may not be your birthday, but it is the anniversary of my parent's wedding, and the first day of my belief in an afterlife."

SCOTTDALE SPOOKIES

The following vignettes are stories told to me by local folks who prefer not to be identified. But they came across as honest and sincere when they told me of events they had experienced. And they agreed to allow me to include them in this book.

1) There is a road near the St Joseph's cemetery; and along that road there used to be a bar. It is rumored that several years ago a man was murdered outside that bar. Friends of mine have been avoiding that road at night. On two occasions, when they were driving near the site of the former bar they have seen a hazy, smoky, humanoid form appear suddenly in the front of their car. On both occasions the driver swerved to avoid the apparition and nearly wrecked. They wonder if the murdered man is seeking company!
2) A former employee of the Southmoreland School District told me he saw a red-haired woman walk in front of him down one of the halls in the high school but then vanish when she walked through a wall! He

says he thinks he may have seen the spirit of a former teacher who died suddenly at a young age. He said that in life she had a fiery disposition to match her flaming hair; so he suspects she is to blame for doors slamming in the school despite the absence of any living human nearby.

3) A woman whose husband abandoned her and their daughters told me of this eerie experience she had many years later. She said that her husband had lost his job. They got into an argument about finances; he left the house and was never heard from again. She raised the girls, managing by working at a variety of part-time jobs. Eventually all three of the children grew up and took up lives as adults. The event she told me about occurred some twenty-five years after her husband's disappearance. She said she got a phone call from him. His voice sounded distant, but there was no doubt in her mind that it was he. He cried and told her how sorry and remorseful he was for abandoning her and the girls. He said he wanted to come home but couldn't. He cried, sounding anguished. She told him he was welcome to come home—that she still lived in the same apartment and still loved him. Through tears and sobs he told her he still loved her, too. Then there was a lot of static on the line and the connection ended. Two hours later she

had another phone call. This one was from a medical examiner in Las Vegas. He said a homeless man in his sixties had been found dead on the street the previous evening. The man had had her name and phone number in his wallet. She realized that her husband had contacted her after death to make amends.

4) The woman who told me about this experience is now elderly. But she says the event is still vivid in her mind. She was taking part in a music recital in the local Lutheran church on Mulberry Street. The participants were all music students of the late Margaret Kritchgau. Near the end of the recital for reasons she does not remember, the lights were turned off briefly, leaving the church in darkness. And that is when she had her "vision" of a young man. His features were distorted by pain and anguish but she could see that he had dark hair and a husky build, and he looked like a fellow she knew slightly. She was sitting in the second pew from the front and the image was on the floor in front of the pulpit. The lights were out no more than thirty seconds; and when they came back on there was nothing out of the ordinary to be seen in the church. The recital ended shortly thereafter. As she left the church with her parents the shriek of an ambulance siren could be heard in the distance. The next day she learned that a young man

she knew, who worked in a local gas station, had gotten his leg broken at work. And she realized that the image she had seen was of this young man. That young man is also quite old now. If he reads this story, he is likely to recognize himself—but not the young woman who "saw" him in the church.

5) This experience took place in Pittsburgh, but to a Scottdale woman. She said she belonged to a church bowling league that played on Saturday evenings. One night as she was putting on her bowling shoes the seventeen-year-old son of another bowling couple walked by and the thought crossed her mind that the boy was dead. But she shook off that bizarre thought and only remembered it two days later when the boy was killed by a speeding truck as he walked across the street to the high school.

MAY I HAVE THIS DANCE

This is a true story. It happened to my daughter a few years ago.

My daughter, Patricia, had an experience recently that was paranormal in nature. She was browsing Facebook and came across the page of a woman, Susan, with whom she had been friends in childhood. Our family had moved from Pittsburgh to California when the girls were about twelve years old and the two of them had not had contact since that time. On Susan's Facebook page was a picture of her father, honoring him for Father's Day and indicating he had died fifteen years earlier.

As my daughter gazed at the photo of Susan's father she was flooded with memories of him from her childhood. In fact, some of these memories were of incidences and events that she had not recalled in many years. She said she felt as though she were in an altered state of consciousness. As Patricia stared at the photo of Susan's father she felt in her mind that the man stretched out his hand, as though to grasp my daughter's. But then she "saw" Susan's mother take the father's hand. The couple smiled at each another and began to dance to a 70's tune that my daughter remembered only vaguely. It was titled, "May I Have This Dance?"

Patricia wrote on Susan's Facebook page about her memories of Susan's father, but did not mention the imaging of Susan's mother and father together. She chose not to share the latter part of her reverie with Susan because she feared Susan might think Patricia had become mentally deranged in the years since they had been children together. Susan responded that Patricia had captured her father perfectly and expressed amazement that Patricia had remembered the man so well. At the time, Susan's mother was alive and well. But a week later Susan contacted my daughter to tell her that her mother, always in fine health, had just had a massive stroke and had died. Patricia still did not tell Susan about her mental image of the dancing parents because she no longer knew Susan well enough to be certain how she might react to such a communication.

But shortly afterward Susan commented on Facebook that she had heard from an old childhood friend named Nancy, who told Susan that she had opened a drawer at home and found a picture of Susan and her parents that had been taken in 1978. Nancy added that it meant to her that Susan's parents were together and that Susan remained joined with them. Susan told Patricia that she was comforted by Nancy's comments.

Bolstered by Susan's attitude, Patricia then told Susan about her vivid imagery. Susan responded that she knew my daughter had experienced a true communication because her parents used to dance in the kitchen to "their" song, which was, "May I Have this Dance?"

THE ROYAL

As of this writing she is a bright and jolly 101 years old. This story, a work of fiction, is written to honor my sister, who has been supportive and accepting of me throughout my life.

The aging children, all in their seventies, had just buried their one hundred seven-year-old mother. As they sorted through her possessions, David found the wrinkled, yellowed letter in his mother's purse and read it to his siblings:

november, 2020/june, 1941

dear bubs, i hope i can complete this letter to you before the ribbon runs out of ink or some other disaster interferes. i think i am in a coma, dying of the covid virus. The covid-19 virus, as it is called, has caused a world-wide pandemic this year, very much as did the spanish flu of 1918 that killed some of our relatives. the last thing i can remember, before i became a small child again, was being very sick and in the hospital. but for the past several days i find i am my former three-year-old self with a memory of my entire life to come---because i have already lived it. i tried to tell you about my circumstances a few days ago but my babyish voice doesn’t translate well. when you grasped some of what i was trying to tell you, you patiently explained déjà vu to me—but this aint déjà vu, honey.

i tried to write down my situation with a paper and pencil you gave me, but my childish scrawl was illegible, even to me. then i remembered your royal typewriter, and am giving it a try. the keys are so hard to push effectively that i have to use my thumbs. there is no way for me to use capitalization appropriately, because i can’t depress the shift key and a letter at the same time. it takes two hands for me to use the carriage return lever-it is a real b----. as you can see, i was able to manage the paper table and roller knob. what i wouldn't give for an old-fashioned word processor—but you probably don't know what that is. anyway, here is the situation. i want to thank you for your love and support over my eighty-some years of life as your sister. And i want to pass along my memories of your very long life, in the hopes that you can be spared some of the anxiety that always accompanies life's uncertainties. at this moment in my other reality you are about to turn a hundred and one years old and are still sharp-minded and witty. i would guess you have a few good years left in you. if i am dying, as i suspect from this strange phenomenon i am experiencing, you will be sad. but i hope this letter will be reassuring. in about six months-in december of 1941, the japanese will bomb a u.s navy base on one of the hawaiian islands. as a result, america will become embroiled in a war that will become known as world war 2. right now you are a school teacher, and after the war you will continue to teach until retirement in your sixties. but you will take a hiatus to serve in the war as a member of the waves, i.e., women accepted for voluntary emergency service. This is a part of the navy that will be created next year. you will be part of an extended navy family—your husband will have served in the navy and one of your sons will graduate from the u.s. military academy. you will be widowed in your early fifties but will cope with that grief. one of your comforts will be your religious faith. i know as i type that you are a closet atheist, despite our family's strong baptist influence. but you are destined to find faith and strength as a mormon. no, i am not joking. you will become a devout mormon, although nowadays the group frowns on the use of that word and prefers saints----latter-day saints. i know you have always preferred non-fiction reading, but do read to kill a mockingbird by an author named harper lee after it gets published. you will have adequate financial resources over the years, but you can brighten your financial picture considerably if you invest in apple

When he finished, Mary laughed, and commented:

"Aunt Margie always liked to write weird stories and this, no doubt, is one of her wild creations from years ago. Funny, though. You know, Mom did invest in an apple company in Oregon several years ago. But I don't think she made anything on the deal."

John was silent for a few minutes, but then commented, as though to himself:

"How would she know she was going to die in November of 2020?"

A CHAT WITH LOUIS

An obvious fiction. With Covid-19 ravaging the globe, this scientist's work with a variety of pathogens has recaptured my interest.

When I saw the bearded man in 1800s period dress, I felt the urge to meet him. I was on a tour bus in Los Angeles and the bus had stopped outside a performance theater for the usual tourist pictures. He was sitting on a bench near a sign that advertised a play called, "An Evening with Louis Pasteur." Exiting the bus, I approached the fellow, who confirmed that he did have a part in the play—as the title character. I explained that I was a visitor from Pennsylvania and that I had a longstanding appreciation of Louis Pasteur. I inquired whether or not the actor had familiarized himself with Pasteur's life in order to get to know his character. Chuckling, he replied that he had worked hard at trying to understand the man but wasn't sure he had succeeded. As he spoke I realized he was "in character," actually speaking English with a decided French accent.

"I have always been grateful to Dr. Pasteur", I confided. "In 1906, on his very first day of school, my father was bitten by a rabid dog. If it had not been for Pasteur's development of the rabies vaccine my father would have died a horrible death and I would not be here. In fact, my father was the first person west of the Allegheny Mountains to receive the Pasteur treatment. Dad remembered the experience clearly even though he was not quite six years old at the time. He said he was hospitalized for weeks, received painful injections into his abdomen. Fortunately, the vaccine has been greatly improved nowadays."

"But what is used nowadays is really no better that the original vaccine", the actor huffed.

"Well, I can't judge that," I responded, somewhat taken aback by his vehemence.

"But the man certainly was an excellent physician and researcher", I added, attempting to maintain a pleasantry between the two of us, despite his off-putting manner.

"Pasteur was not a physician!" The actor was indignant at my gaff. "He was a chemist and microbiologist. And he probably did more to save mankind with his procedure for killing microbes in milk than he did with his vaccines for anthrax and rabies. However, I am, of course, delighted that your father benefitted from the vaccine."

I commented that, with the development of sterile surgical techniques and antibiotics, nowadays many people survive infections that would have killed them in the past. The actor replied with some sadness,

"Nevertheless, as it appears nowadays, 'C'est les microbes qui auront le dernier moi.'"

My response was an erudite, "Huh?"

"Oh, pardon, madame, I forget that you Americans fail to educate yourselves properly in languages other than your own. I said it appears that despite mankind's efforts, microbes will have the last word."

That silenced me. Indeed, in the last several years it did appear that, despite all of our modern vaccines and antibiotic drugs, diseases such as AIDS, MERSA, SARS, Ebola, Legionnaire's Disease and lethal influenzas were flourishing. Mulling this over, I nearly asked the actor if he had any ideas of how modern medicine might better deal with the increase in infectious illnesses. Apparently, I had begun to join in his world of make-believe. But when I opened my mouth to speak he told me I should hurry so as not to be abandoned by my motorized vehicle. I turned to see the bus driver starting the engine. Bidding the actor a hasty farewell, I boarded the bus and the sightseeing tour continued. But I could not get my mind off the actor and his comments. I made up my mind to return to the theater that evening and take in the play. I figured I could learn more about Louis Pasteur and might have a chance to chat again with the very interesting actor.

But when I got back to the theater several hours later, "An Evening with Louis Pasteur" was not playing. The sign I had seen that morning was gone. In its place was an advertisement for that evening's performance of "Heaven Can Wait." When I inquired, the fellow in the box office said that, to the best of his knowledge, "An Evening with Louis Pasteur" had never been a theatrical production.

It was with awe and just a hint of smugness that I realized that I had chatted with the spirit of Louis Pasteur himself.

THE CAR WRECK

Another work of fiction, written several years ago, before I returned in Pennsylvania.

It was about eight o'clock on Saturday morning in central Pennsylvania, and I was enjoying the drive along a mountain ridge on Route 22. The autumn sun was reflecting off the reds and yellows of leaves. My thoughts were on my upcoming visit with my daughter Laura, who lived near Ebensburg.

So, when I first saw the little boy I thought he was just a figment of my imagination. But a glance in the rear view mirror revealed that, indeed, a boy of three or four years old was crouched on the berm of the road. I stopped the car and hurried back to the child. No adults or vehicles were in evidence. As I approached him, he sobbed,

"Help my mommy—she's down there."

Glancing to where the child was pointing, I saw that mountain laurel and small maple trees were broken in an eight-foot swatch leading over the mountainside. About a hundred feet below I could see an edge of blue metal. With horror I realized that this little boy must have been in a car that had gone over the roadside. Somehow the child had managed to climb up the side of the mountain.

"What is your name?" I inquired.

"Jewemy", he responded.

"Is your mommy in the car?" I asked.

He uttered a quivery, "Yes."

The child's face was tearstained and filthy; his blue denims were stained with grass and mud.

"Are you hurting anywhere?" I inquired.

He shook his head.

"I am going to get help for your Mommy", I told him. "How about you walk back to my car with me?"

But he refused, insisting,

"Just get help for my mommy!"

Then he sat back down on the side of the road and crossed his arms in a determined pose that reminded me of a stubborn adult. I told him to sit still and not go near the paved highway. Then I hurried back to my Mercury.

A glance at my cell phone revealed NO SERVICE and I got only a high-pitched repetitive "beep" when I tried to dial 911.

"Darned mountain,"

I mumbled to myself and trudged back to where I had left the child. But he was not there. I called, "Jeremy"

but got no response. Probably the tyke had climbed back down the hillside to be with his mother. Briefly I considered climbing down also, but reason prevailed. What good would I be if I broke an ankle in the process? I realized I could lose fifteen or twenty precious minutes waiting for another vehicle to meander by. Ebensburg was only about fifteen miles further east.

So I drove off, located a local Sheetz mini-mart and was on the phone to the state police within twenty minutes. I rode with the responding state trooper back up the mountain to show him exactly where the car had gone over the embankment. I explained about Jeremy, who still was nowhere to be seen. After an ambulance, tow truck, and two more patrol cars arrived, the officer drove me back to my car at Sheetz. I gave him Laura's phone number, and explained that I would be in the Ebensburg area for the next several days. The state patrolman said he'd get in touch with me if he had further questions.

Several hours later I got a call from the state police substation—could I drop by, because they did have a few more questions. I went immediately. The interviewing officer looked quite serious and asked me to make a formal statement describing everything I had seen and heard on the mountain that morning. I did so, with some uneasiness. Did he think I had caused the wreck? Did he think I had abducted Jeremy? Finally he seemed to run out of questions. He commented that some of my story was confusing. The officer went on to say that the female driver, an Alicia Sommers from Pittsburgh, was in Altoona Hospital with major injuries and severe dehydration. But she was conscious and was expected to pull through. She told the police that on Thursday evening she and her four-year-old son Jeremy were planning a surprise visit to her mother in Cresson when she lost control of her Chrysler and slid over the side of the mountain. Alicia's husband is with the Marines in Afghanistan. So no one was aware that they were missing. I commented that I was relieved that Jeremy's mother was going to recover, but I didn't know what was confusing. Had they not found the child? The state trooper stared at me for a solid minute before answering.

"Oh, yes, we found the boy. He had been thrown out of the car and his body was underneath it. He was probably killed instantly."

I sat in numb disbelief as the trooper went on:

> "I don't know what made you stop your car up there lady, but lucky for the Sommers woman you did. The wreck wasn't visible from the road, and she wouldn't

have lasted much longer. But it sure wasn't the kid you saw by the side of the road."

Well, I knew it was the kid I saw. Or his spirit. But I didn't believe arguing with the state trooper was likely to gain me anything but a short stay in the local loony bin. So I told the officer I didn't know what I had seen either. And I took my leave.

That dear child had saved his mother's life. But why did he show himself to me and not to some other driver? Surely, I wasn't the first driver to pass the site of the wreckage. Did little Jeremy's ghost have to struggle all day Friday to get up the steep hillside? Was the attention of other drivers focused elsewhere so that they failed to see the little boy by the side of the road? I guess I will never really know why I saw Jeremy. But I remain in awe of that courageous and determined little boy who, in death, managed to save his mommy's life. And I am forever grateful for that mysterious glimpse of life after life granted to me one Saturday morning in October.

BRANDON

For this final story, I will leave it up to the reader to decide—fact or fiction?

As we were eating for the first time in a Mexican restaurant that had opened recently, my daughter, her husband and I were talking animatedly about the original brick walls in the restaurant, speculating on what the building had housed in the past. My four-year-old grandson, sounding somewhat like a museum docent, spoke up and said:

> "In 1916 that wall (pointing) was open and the horses would come in and pull the fire carriages behind them. Then the horses would be put over there (pointing to another part of the restaurant) and the wagons would sit about here (indicating the area in which we were sitting.)" I was dumbfounded and said,

"1916?"

I was questioning not the issue of the year but pondering how a four-year-old would know there had BEEN such a year. Apparently thinking I was doubting the accuracy of his narrative, Brandon said,

> "Well, it could have been 1917 or 1918 but I think it was in 1916."

Then, Brandon went on, using mature words and demeanor, as he reported on the firehouse dogs and their role in helping the firemen. The three adults at the table sat in bewildered silence until the owner of the restaurant, came by to inquire after our satisfaction. My daughter asked her if she knew the history of the structure. The woman said she knew it was built in the 1800s, had housed several businesses, one of which had been a fire station.

Again, we adults were silent, communicating only with nervous glances. We paid our bill and returned to the car. On the way home I asked Brandon how he had known the building we just left had been a firehouse with horses. He didn't answer me directly but said, sounding sad,

> "Around 1923 they brought in gas engines and quit using horses on the fire trucks, and shortly after that they got ladder trucks."

My daughter asked him if he used to work in the fire station. (With the active imagination not rare in a preschooler, Brandon is always telling us he worked here or there.) But he told her that he hadn't worked at the firehouse, and that he had only moved "down to Bakersfield from Merced" when he was sixty years old. Merced is a town around one hundred miles north of Bakersfield. Brandon has never been there, we know no one who lives there, and it is unlikely the town has ever come up in conversation in the house. My daughter asked Brandon how he could have been old and now be only four years old. He said he didn't know and that "it just happened."

Just as weird as the above report: About five minutes after the last part of Brandon's dialogue, his father asked him when he had heard of Merced. The child seemed to be confused and told his father he didn't know what his father meant. And he denied ever saying the word.

To add more intrigue to all of this, the name of the restaurant we had been dining in that evening is named "Muertos" which is "The Dead Ones" in Spanish.

ABOUT THE AUTHOR

Marjorie Osterwise TaVoularis, MD, PhD, is a retired physician and board-certified psychiatrist. Born and raised in Scottdale, PA, she returned there to live for another twelve years after spending more than twenty-five years in California. Several of those West Coast years were spent working in jails and prisons. She recently retired to Las Vegas, Nevada. She is the mother of four daughters (one deceased), a grandmother of three children and a great-grandmother of two boys.

Made in United States
Orlando, FL
13 September 2022

22373849R00050